KU-165-627

Ladybird books are widely available, but in case of
difficulty may be ordered by post or telephone from:

Ladybird Books–Cash Sales Department
Littlegate Road Paignton Devon TQ3 3BE
Telephone 01803 554761

A catalogue record for this book is available
from the British Library

Published by Ladybird Books Ltd Loughborough Leicestershire UK
Ladybird Books Inc Auburn Maine 04210 USA

NONSENSE RHYME

BY EDWARD LEAR

Selected by Ronne Randall
Illustrated by John Lawrence

Edward Lear
was born in 1812 and died in 1888.
He is best known for his humorous verse,
particularly his limericks. He was also
an accomplished artist, specialising in
watercolours of animals and landscapes.
In fact, his artistic skills were so highly thought of
that he once gave drawing lessons to
Queen Victoria!

Contents

They went to sea in a Sieve

THE JUMBLIES

They went to sea in a Sieve, they did,
   In a Sieve they went to sea:
In spite of all their friends could say,
On a winter's morn, on a stormy day,
   In a Sieve they went to sea!
And when the Sieve turned round and round,
And everyone cried, 'You'll all be drowned!'
They called aloud, 'Our Sieve ain't big,
But we don't care a button! we don't care a fig!
   In a Sieve we'll go to sea!'
     Far and few, far and few,
       Are the lands where the Jumblies live;
       Their heads are green, and their hands are blue,
       And they went to sea in a Sieve.

They sailed away in a Sieve, they did,

    In a Sieve they sailed so fast,

With only a beautiful pea-green veil

Tied with a riband by way of a sail,

    To a small tobacco-pipe mast;

And everyone said, who saw them go,

'O won't they be soon upset, you know!

For the sky is dark, and the voyage is long,

And happen what may, it's extremely wrong

    In a Sieve to sail so fast!'

      Far and few, far and few,

        Are the lands where the Jumblies live;

      Their heads are green, and their hands are blue,

        And they went to sea in a Sieve.

The water it soon came in, it did,

　The water it soon came in;

So to keep them dry, they wrapped their feet

In a pinky paper all folded neat,

　And they fastened it down with a pin.

And they passed the night in a crockery-jar,

And each of them said, 'How wise we are!

Though the sky be dark, and the voyage be long,

Yet we never can think we were rash or wrong,

　While round in our Sieve we spin!'

　　Far and few, far and few,

　　　Are the lands where the Jumblies live;

　　Their heads are green, and their hands are blue,

　　　And they went to sea in a Sieve.

And all night long they sailed away;

    And when the sun went down,

They whistled and warbled a moony song

To the echoing sound of a coppery gong,

    In the shade of the mountains brown.

'O Timballoo! How happy we are,

When we live in a sieve and a crockery-jar,

And all night long in the moonlight pale,

We sail away with a pea-green sail,

    In the shade of the mountains brown!'

      Far and few, far and few,

        Are the lands where the Jumblies live;

       Their heads are green, and their hands are blue,

        And they went to sea in a Sieve.

And all night long they sailed away

They sailed to the Western Sea, they did,

   To a land all covered with trees,

And they bought an Owl, and a useful Cart,

And a pound of Rice, and a Cranberry Tart,

   And a hive of silvery Bees.

And they bought a Pig, and some green Jackdaws,

And a lovely Monkey with lollipop paws,

And forty bottles of Ring-Bo-Ree,

   And no end of Stilton Cheese.

    Far and few, far and few,

      Are the lands where the Jumblies live;

     Their heads are green, and their hands are blue,

      And they went to sea in a Sieve.

And in twenty years they all came back,

   In twenty years or more,

And everyone said, 'How tall they've grown!

For they've been to the Lakes, and the Torrible Zone,

   And the hills of the Chankly Bore!'

     Far and few, far and few,

      Are the lands where the Jumblies live;

     Their heads are green, and their hands are blue,

      And they went to sea in a Sieve.

There was an Old Man on whose nose...

LIMERICKS

There was an Old Man on whose nose,
Most birds of the air could repose;
   But they all flew away,
   At the closing of day,
Which relieved that Old Man and his nose.

There was an Old Lady of France,
Who taught little Ducklings to dance;
   When she said: 'Tick-a-tack!',
   They only said, 'Quack!',
Which grieved that Old Lady of France.

There was an Old Person of Dover,
Who rushed through a field of blue clover;
    But some very large bees,
    Stung his nose and his knees,
So he very soon went back to Dover.

There was an Old Man of the Hague,
Whose ideas were excessively vague;
    He built a balloon,
    To examine the moon,
That deluded old man of the Hague.

There was an Old Man of Coblenz,
The length of whose legs was immense;
    He went with one prance,
    From Turkey to France,
That surprising Old Man of Coblenz.

THE COURTSHIP
OF THE
YONGHY-BONGHY-BÒ

On the Coast of Coromandel
Where the early pumpkins blow,
In the middle of the woods
Lived the Yonghy-Bonghy-Bò.
Two old chairs, and half a candle, –
One old jug without a handle, –
These were all his worldly goods:
In the middle of the woods,
These were all the worldly goods,
Of the Yonghy-Bonghy-Bò,
Of the Yonghy-Bonghy-Bò.

Once, among the Bong-trees walking
Where the early pumpkins blow,
To a little heap of stones
Came the Yonghy-Bonghy-Bò.
There he heard a Lady talking,
To some milk-white Hens of Dorking, –
''Tis the Lady Jingly Jones!
On that little heap of stones
Sits the Lady Jingly Jones!'
Said the Yonghy-Bonghy-Bò,
Said the Yonghy-Bonghy-Bò.

'Tis the Lady Jingly Jones!'

'Lady Jingly! Lady Jingly!
    Sitting where the pumpkins blow,
        Will you come and be my wife?'
    Said the Yonghy-Bonghy-Bò.
'I am tired of living singly, –
On this coast so wild and shingly, –
        I'm a-weary of my life:
        If you'll come and be my wife,
        Quite serene would be my life!' –
    Said the Yonghy-Bonghy-Bò,
    Said the Yonghy-Bonghy-Bò.

'On this Coast of Coromandel,
   Shrimps and watercresses grow,
      Prawns are plentiful and cheap,'
   Said the Yonghy-Bonghy-Bò.
'You shall have my Chairs and candle,
And my jug without a handle! –
      Gaze upon the rolling deep
      (Fish is plentiful and cheap)
      As the sea, my love is deep!'
   Said the Yonghy-Bonghy-Bò,
   Said the Yonghy-Bonghy-Bò.

'Your proposal comes too late'

Lady Jingly answered sadly,

   And her tears began to flow, –

     'Your proposal comes too late,

   Mr Yonghy-Bonghy-Bò!

I would be your wife most gladly!'

(Here she twirled her fingers madly,)

     'But in England I've a mate!

     Yes! you've asked me far too late,

     For in England I've a mate,

   Mr Yonghy-Bonghy-Bò!

   Mr Yonghy-Bonghy-Bò!'

'Mr Jones – (his name is Handel, –

    Handel Jones, Esquire, & Co)

        Dorking fowls delights to send,

    Mr Yonghy-Bonghy-Bò!

Keep, oh! keep your chairs and candle,

And your jug without a handle, –

        I can merely be your friend!

        – Should my Jones more Dorkings send,

        I will give you three, my friend!

    Mr Yonghy-Bonghy-Bò!

    Mr Yonghy-Bonghy-Bò!

'Though you've such a tiny body,

   And your head so large doth grow, –

     Though your hat may blow away,

   Mr Yonghy-Bonghy-Bò!

Though you're such a Hoddy Doddy –

Yet I wish that I could modi-

     fy the words I needs must say!

     Will you please to go away?

     That is all I have to say –

   Mr Yonghy-Bonghy-Bò!

   Mr Yonghy-Bonghy-Bò!'

Down the slippery slopes of Myrtle,

   Where the early pumpkins blow,

    To the calm and silent sea

   Fled the Yonghy-Bonghy-Bò.

There, beyond the Bay of Gurtle,

Lay a large and lively Turtle; –

     'You're the Cove,' he said, 'for me

     On your back beyond the sea,

     Turtle, you shall carry me!'

   Said the Yonghy-Bonghy-Bò,

   Said the Yonghy-Bonghy-Bò.

'Turtle, you shall carry me!'

Through the silent-roaring ocean
    Did the Turtle swiftly go;
        Holding fast upon his shell
    Rode the Yonghy-Bonghy-Bò.
With a sad primæval motion
Towards the sunset isles of Boshen
        Still the Turtle bore him well.
        Holding fast upon his shell,
        'Lady Jingly Jones, farewell!'
    Sang the Yonghy-Bonghy-Bò.
    Sang the Yonghy-Bonghy-Bò.

From the Coast of Coromandel,

    Did that Lady never go;

        On that heap of stones she mourns

    For the Yonghy-Bonghy-Bò.

On that Coast of Coromandel,

In his jug without a handle

        Still she weeps and daily moans;

        On that little heap of stones

        To her Dorking Hens she moans,

    For the Yonghy-Bonghy-Bò,

    For the Yonghy-Bonghy-Bò.

There was an Old Man of Aosta

MORE LIMERICKS

There was an Old Man of Aosta,
Who possessed a large cow, but he lost her;
   But they said: 'Don't you see
   She has rushed up a tree?
You invidious Old Man of Aosta!'

There was an Old Man of Peru
Who never knew what he should do;
   So he sat on a chair,
   And behaved liked a bear,
That unhappy Old Man of Peru.

There was a Young Lady of Dorking,

Who bought a large bonnet for walking;

    But its colour and size,

    So bedazzled her eyes,

That she very soon went back to Dorking.

There was an Old Man of the South

Who had an immoderate mouth;

    But in swallowing a dish

    Which was quite full of fish,

He was choked – that Old Man of the South.

There was an Old Man of Berlin,

Whose form was uncommonly thin,

    Till he once, by mistake,

    Was mixed up in a cake,

So they baked the old man of Berlin.

THE POBBLE
WHO HAS NO TOES

The Pobble who has no toes
  Had once as many as we;
When they said, 'Some day you may lose them all' –
  He replied, 'Fish fiddle de-dee!'
And his Aunt Jobiska made him drink,
Lavender water tinged with pink,
For she said, 'The World in general knows
There's nothing so good for a Pobble's toes!'

The Pobble who has no toes,
  Swam across the Bristol Channel;
But before he set out he wrapped his nose,
  In a piece of scarlet flannel.
For his Aunt Jobiska said, 'No harm
Can come to his toes if his nose is warm;
And it's perfectly known that a Pobble's toes
Are safe – provided he minds his nose.'

The Pobble swam fast and well
    And when boats or ships came near him
He tinkledy-binkledy-winkled a bell
    So that all the world could hear him.
And all the Sailors and Admirals cried,
When they saw him nearing the further side –
'He has gone to fish, for his Aunt Jobiska's
Runcible Cat with crimson whiskers!'

But before he touched the shore,
    The shore of the Bristol Channel,
A sea-green Porpoise carried away
    His wrapper of scarlet flannel.
And when he came to observe his feet
Formerly garnished with toes so neat
His face at once became forlorn
On perceiving that all his toes were gone!

All his toes were gone!

And nobody ever knew

    From that dark day to the present,

Whoso had taken the Pobble's toes,

    In a manner so far from pleasant.

Whether the shrimps or crawfish grey,

Or crafty Mermaids stole them away –

Nobody; and nobody knows

How the Pobble was robbed of his twice five toes!

The Pobble who has no toes

    Was placed in a friendly Bark,

And they rowed him back, and carried him up,

    To his Aunt Jobiska's Park.

And she made him a feast at his earnest wish

Of eggs and buttercups fried with fish –

And she said, 'It's a fact the whole world knows,

That Pobbles are happier without their toes.'

STILL MORE LIMERICKS

There was an Old Man of Dumbree,
Who taught little owls to drink tea;
   For he said, 'To eat mice,
   Is not proper or nice,'
That amiable Man of Dumbree.

There was an Old Person of Tring,
Who embellished his nose with a ring;
   He gazed at the moon
   Every evening in June,
That ecstatic Old Person of Tring.

There was a Young Lady of Bute

There was an Old Man who made bold
To affirm that the weather was cold;
　　So he ran up and down,
　　In his grandmother's gown,
Which was woollen, and not very old.

There was a Young Lady of Bute,
Who played on a silver-gilt flute;
　　She played several jigs,
　　To her uncle's white pigs,
That amusing Young Lady of Bute.

There was an Old Person of Rheims,
Who was troubled by horrible dreams;
　　So to keep him awake,
　　They fed him with cake,
That afflicted Old Person of Rheims!

THE QUANGLE WANGLE'S HAT

On top of the Crumpetty Tree
   The Quangle Wangle sat,
But his face you could not see,
   On account of his Beaver Hat.
For his Hat was a hundred and two feet wide,
With ribbons and bibbons on every side,
And bells, and buttons, and loops, and lace,
So that nobody ever could see the face
   Of the Quangle Wangle Quee.

The Quangle Wangle said
     To himself on the Crumpetty Tree,
'Jam, and jelly, and bread
     Are the best of food for me!
But the longer I live on this Crumpetty Tree
The plainer than ever it seems to me
That very few people come this way
And that life on the whole is far from gay!'
     Said the Quangle Wangle Quee.

But there came to the Crumpetty Tree
     Mr and Mrs Canary;
And they said, 'Did you ever see
     Any spot so charmingly airy?
May we build a nest on your lovely Hat?
Mr Quangle Wangle, grant us that!
Oh, please let us come and build a nest,
Of whatever material suits you best,
     Mr Quangle Wangle Quee!'

And besides, to the Crumpetty Tree

    Came the Stork, the Duck, and the Owl;

The Snail and the Bumble Bee,

    The Frog and the Fimble Fowl

(The Fimble Fowl, with a corkscrew leg);

And all of them said, 'We humbly beg

We may build our homes on your lovely Hat –

Mr Quangle Wangle, grant us that!

    Mr Quangle Wangle Quee!'

And the Golden Grouse came there,

    And the Pobble who has no toes,

And the small Olympian Bear,

    And the Dong with a luminous nose.

And the Blue Baboon who played the flute,

And the Orient Calf from the Land of Tute,

And the Attery Squash, and the Bisky Bat –

All came and built on the lovely Hat

    Of the Quangle Wangle Quee!

All came and built on the lovely Hat

And the Quangle Wangle said

 To himself on the Crumpetty Tree,
'When all these creatures move

 What a wonderful noise there'll be!'
And at night by the light of the Mulberry Moon
They danced to the Flute of the Blue Baboon,
On the broad green leaves of the Crumpetty Tree,
And all were as happy as happy could be,

 With the Quangle Wangle Quee.

EVEN MORE LIMERICKS

There was an Old Lady of Chertsey,

Who made a remarkable curtsey;

    She twirled round and round,

    Till she sank underground,

Which distressed all the people of Chertsey.

There was an Old Person of Anerley,

Whose conduct was strange and unmannerly;

    He rushed down the Strand,

    With a Pig in each hand,

But returned in the evening to Anerley.

There was an Old Man with a beard

There was a Young Lady of Hull,
Who was chased by a virulent Bull;
    But she caught up a spade,
    And called out, 'Who's afraid?'
That remarkable Lady of Hull.

There was an Old Man with a beard,
Who said, 'It is just as I feared! –
    Two Owls and a Hen,
    Four Larks and a Wren,
Have all built their nests in my beard!'

There was an Old Man of the North,
Who fell into a basin of broth;
    But a laudable cook,
    Fished him out with a hook,
Which saved that Old Man of the North.

THE OWL
AND THE PUSSY-CAT

The Owl and the Pussy-cat went to sea
   In a beautiful pea-green boat,
They took some honey, and plenty of money,
   Wrapped up in a five-pound note.
The Owl looked up to the stars above,
   And sang to a small guitar,
'O lovely Pussy! O Pussy, my love,
     What a beautiful Pussy you are,
      You are,
      You are!
     What a beautiful Pussy you are!'

Pussy said to the Owl, 'You elegant fowl!

　　How charmingly sweet you sing!

O let us be married! too long we have tarried:

　　But what shall we do for a ring?'

They sailed away, for a year and a day,

　　To the land where the Bong-tree grows

And there in a wood a Piggy-wig stood

　　　With a ring at the end of his nose,

　　　　His nose,

　　　　His nose,

　　　With a ring at the end of his nose.

They danced by the light of the moon

'Dear Pig, are you willing to sell for one shilling
   Your ring?' Said the Piggy, 'I will.'
So they took it away, and were married next day
   By the turkey who lives on the hill.
They dined on mince, and slices of quince,
   Which they ate with a runcible spoon;
And hand in hand, on the edge of the sand,
     They danced by the light of the moon,
      The moon,
      The moon,
     They danced by the light of the moon.